Jason
04. 02. 04

Die.

Mr. Clumsy

Mr. Daydream

Mr. Chatterbox

little Miss Fickle

Mr. Mischief

Mr. Uppity

Mr. Dizzy

little Miss Somersault

Mr. Greedy

little Miss Scatterbrain

Mr. Mean

little Miss Stubborn

little Miss Magic

Mr. Tickle

mr. Happy

little Miss Greedy

Mr. Sneeze

mr. Nosey

little Miss Twins

Mr. Strong

Mr. Grumble

Mr. Bump

Mr. Forgetful

little Miss Cc

MR MEN and LITTLE MISS™& © 1999 Mrs Roger Hargreaves.
All rights reserved. Printed and published 1999 under licence
from Price Stern Sloan Inc., Los Angeles. Stories first published in
the 1997, 1998 and 1999 Mr Men and Little Miss Annuals.
This story collection published in Great Britain by Egmont World Ltd.,
Deanway Technology Centre, Wilmslow Road,
Handforth, Cheshire, SK9 3FB.
Printed in Italy.
Hardback ISBN 0 7498 4356 X
Paperback ISBN 0 7498 4413 2

MR. MEN
AND
little Miss

Roger Hargreaves

A Bedtime Story Book

Original concept by Roger Hargreaves

Illustrated by Adam and Giles Hargreaves

New text written by John Malam

Designed by Dave Murray

Cover designed by Julie Morris

This Bedtime Story Book belongs to:

....

I am .... years old

Contents

Ssshh! Quiet please!

Mr Chatterbox was talking to Mr Grumble. He was doing enough talking for both of them. Each time Mr Grumble tried to say something, Mr Chatterbox thought of something else to say.

"Ah-hem!" said Mr Grumble.

"And as I was saying," continued Mr Chatterbox.

"Bah!" said Mr Grumble.

Just then, Mr Mischief came along. "Hello," he said. "Lovely day for a chat."

"Bah!" said Mr Grumble. "It might be a lovely day to you, but I've been waiting for ages to say something to Mr Chatterbox!"

At which point, Mr Chatterbox stopped just long enough for Mr Mischief to tell him that his shoelaces were undone. Which, of course, they were not. That was just Mr Mischief playing a joke on Mr Chatterbox, and also on Mr Grumble.

"Bah!" said Mr Grumble. "It was my turn to speak! Now Mr Chatterbox has started talking again. Just listen to him!"

"Well," said Mr Chatterbox, "if my shoelaces really were undone, it would have been good of you to tell me. Even though they were still tied up tightly, it was worth me checking them, just in case they really were coming loose …"

8

"Bah!" said Mr Grumble, again.

"If I were you," said Mr Mischief, whispering in Mr Grumble's ear, "I'd tell him that today is 'National No Chatting Day'. That might make him stop talking. Then you can say what you want to."

"That'll never work. Not in a month of Sundays," he said, in a grumbling sort of voice.

"Oh, well," said Mr Mischief. "You'll never find out unless you try, will you?" Mr Grumble cleared his throat. "Ah-hem!" he said, loudly, followed by "Bah!"

At which point Mr Chatterbox stopped talking, right in the middle of a word. Very quickly, Mr Grumble explained that today was 'National No Chatting Day', just like Mr Mischief had said.

Mr Chatterbox slowly closed his mouth and swallowed the unfinished word. "Gulp!" he said.

"See, I told you it would work," said Mr Mischief, grinning.

"Ssshh!" said Mr Chatterbox to Mr Mischief. "Quiet please! Don't you know you shouldn't be talking today?"

And with that he was off again, explaining to Mr Grumble all about 'National No Chatting Day'. "I think it's a very good idea for everyone to be quiet today," he said. "I must go and tell as many people as I can!"

"So much for your good idea!" said Mr Grumble to Mr Mischief.

"Tricked you!" said Mr Mischief.

But do you know something? Mr Grumble had the last word after all. "BAH!" he said. What else could it have been?

The broken vase

Mr Dizzy had decided to help Mr Clumsy hang a picture on the wall. But he managed to hang it upside-down. Then Mr Clumsy slipped and pulled it down. He wouldn't have minded, except that it got caught in the curtains and pulled them down too, quickly followed by the curtain pole which just happened to knock a vase of flowers over.

"Phew!" said Mr Clumsy. "It could have been worse. At least the vase didn't break!"

At which point Mr Dizzy picked it up … slipped on the spilled water, fell over and dropped the vase. It broke into pieces.

"Ooops!" said Mr Dizzy. "Sorry."

They picked up the pieces of the broken vase, all sixty-six of them, and put them into a bag.

"If we buy some glue, we can stick the vase together again," said Mr Dizzy.

On the way to the shops they met Mr Wrong. They told him about the broken vase.

"You don't want to use glue," he said. "It'll make a terrible mess. If I were you, I would use toothpaste." Mr Dizzy and Mr Clumsy looked at each other in a funny sort of way. But before they could say anything, Mr Wrong had tipped the bag upside-down. The sixty-six pieces of broken vase fell on to the ground, and smashed into even more pieces. Eighty-eight, to be precise.

"Steady on!" said Mr Clumsy.

"Be careful!" said Mr Dizzy.

"Pardon?" said Mr Wrong, turning even redder than he usually was, and pretending not to hear. In no time at all he'd squeezed toothpaste all over the pieces of broken vase.

"You're making a terrible mess," said Mr Clumsy.

"I don't think the pieces are sticking together at all," said Mr Dizzy.

"Maybe if I used cheese spread instead of toothpaste," said Mr Wrong.

"No thank you!" said Mr Dizzy. "I think I'll stick to glue."

"Very funny!" said Mr Clumsy.

"Pardon?" said Mr Wrong, not sure what was funny at all.

They picked the eighty-eight pieces of broken vase up, put them back in the bag, and carried on walking.

"Just a moment," called out Mr Wrong. "I could use runny honey instead … or sticky toffee … or even gooey marmalade."

But Mr Dizzy and Mr Clumsy didn't think those were very good ideas.

"No thank you," they said.

Do you know what they really used to stick the vase back together? Well I can tell you that it wasn't glue. Oh no, not glue. They used sticky tape. Yards and yards and yards of it.

"Now, why didn't Mr Wrong think of that?" asked Mr Clumsy.

"Why indeed?" said Mr Dizzy.

Well, what would you have used? Go on, tell me!

A very clean house

Mr Forgetful was cleaning his house. "I can't remember when I last cleaned Forget-me-Not Cottage," he said. "Was it yesterday or last week?" He couldn't remember. "Or was it the day before yesterday?"

There was a knock at the door. It was Mr Daydream.

"I was having the most incredible daydream. I imagined you were cleaning your house again, from top to bottom, side to side,

inside and outside – just like you did yesterday!"

"Oh, so that's when I last cleaned my house. I was beginning to wonder," said Mr Forgetful. "Now I've started, I'll have to finish."

Mr Daydream said he would help. But there was a problem. There wasn't a brush for him to use. Guess what he did. He went and asked Mr Mean if he could borrow a brush from him. Would you have done that?

"I never lend my brush to anyone," said Mr Mean, meanly.

"Please," said Mr Daydream. "Just this once."

"No," said Mr Mean, using just one little word. He was mean with everything, words included.

"Go on!" tried Mr Daydream.

Mr Mean said nothing. He just folded his arms, pressed his lips together, narrowed his eyes and shook his head. Once only. And that was it.

He went inside his house and closed the door.

Mr Daydream went back to Mr Forgetful's house. He had gone! Mr Forgetful had tried to make himself a cup of tea. But he had forgotten to put tea leaves into the teapot. He had ended up with a cup of hot water instead.

"Yuck!" he said. "I think something's missing from this cup of tea. What could it be?"

And with that, he went off to the library to look for a book. A book called 'How To Make Tea'. Only when he got there, he couldn't remember what the book was called. "I think I'd better go home," he said.

But when he got back, who should he find inside his house? It was Mr Daydream, of course. And can you guess what he was doing? Mr Forgetful will tell you.

"Why are you cleaning my house?" asked Mr Forgetful.

Mr Daydream explained: "... and when I got back, you weren't here, so I picked your brush up and started cleaning, just like I said I was going to."

"Well," said Mr Forgetful, "I don't remember that. But it was good of you. Thank you."

Then guess what he said. "All that cleaning must have made you thirsty," he said to Mr Daydream. "I'll make us a nice pot of tea."

Now would you drink a cup of tea made by Mr Forgetful?

Yuck! Yuck! Yuck!

The lost handbag

Little Miss Somersault likes to keep fit. In fact, she is the fittest person I know. As soon as she wakes up she does three high jumps in the air, followed by four handstands, and then head over heels, five times.

Now, a few days ago, this is what happened next.

"Today feels like a day for lots of exercise," she said, bending down to touch her toes, six times.

And that was when Little Miss Contrary came running along, out of breath.

"Hello," she said, in a panting sort of a voice. "Have you dropped something?"

"Don't be silly!" said Little Miss Somersault.

"I'm touching my toes because I'm exercising!"

"Does that mean you're also good at running?" asked Little Miss Contrary. "Because if it does, you might be able to help me."

Little Miss Contrary explained that Little Miss Scatterbrain had been to visit her, but had left her handbag behind. "You could run after her. You'll catch her up before I do," she said.

Little Miss Somersault took the handbag and set off to Buttercup Cottage, which was where Little Miss Scatterbrain lived.

Now, if you or I had run that far, it would have taken three and a half minutes. But for Little Miss Somersault it took no time at all.

She knocked on the door. No reply. So she sat down and waited. But you know what Little Miss Somersault is like. She can't sit still for long. She started exercising. Three headstands, four press-ups then five laps of the garden.

"Coo-ee," called a voice. It was Little Miss Scatterbrain. "Here I am. Oh, what a lovely handbag you've got," she said, pointing at the handbag Little Miss Somersault was holding. "I've just bought one exactly the same as yours."

"But," began Little Miss Somersault, "this is your handbag. You left it at Little Miss Contrary's house."

"Oh, did I?" said Little Miss Scatterbrain, in a sheepish sort of a voice. "Wherever I go I leave my handbag behind

and then end up buying another one exactly the same! Then someone brings my old handbag back to me. So now I've got thirty identical handbags, not to mention the forty identical hats, the fifty identical pairs of gloves or the —"

Little Miss Somersault didn't wait to hear the rest of the list. "Sorry, can't stay any longer," she said. "I promised I'd show Little Miss Contrary how to do cartwheels. Bye-bye!" And off she went, cartwheeling all the way back to her house.

Mr Greedy's

"Today's the day at last!" said Mr Greedy. "Today's the day me and my gigantic roly-poly tummy are going to Mr Mischief's house for tea. I do hope there will be lots of sticky strawberry jam sandwiches, wibbly-wobbly jellies and gooey chocolate cakes. I'm feeling hungrier than ever!"

But Mr Greedy was in for a big surprise. He should have known that Mr Mischief liked to play tricks.

It was a very long way to Mr Mischief's house. Mr Greedy began to think that Mr Mischief might start without him, and eat all the food! There would be no sticky strawberry jam sandwiches, no wibbly-wobbly jellies and absolutely no gooey chocolate cakes!

Mr Greedy held on to his tummy and started to run. But he needn't have worried. Mr Mischief hadn't eaten the food. In fact, he hadn't even touched it. So when Mr Greedy saw the table piled high with, you've guessed it, sticky strawberry jam sandwiches, wibbly-wobbly jellies and gooey chocolate cakes, his tummy seemed to grow bigger.

"Can we start now?" asked Mr Greedy, greedily.

Mr Mischief said he wanted Mr Greedy to play a guessing game. He said he wanted Mr Greedy to close his eyes, and try to guess what he was eating.

guessing game

Mr Greedy should have known that Mr Mischief was about to play a trick on him. But all he could think of was the tasty food.

"Close your eyes and open your mouth," said Mr Mischief.

Mr Greedy was expecting Mr Mischief to pop a strawberry jam sandwich into his mouth.

"Uggh!" said Mr Greedy. "That tastes like soggy cornflakes!"

"Let's try something else," said Mr Mischief, trying not to laugh.

Mr Greedy was hoping for a mouthful of jelly. But instead …

 "Yuck! That tastes like cold porridge!" he spluttered.

"One more," said Mr Mischief.

"I hope it's chocolate cake," began Mr Greedy, who then looked startled and said, "Arrgh! It tastes like burnt toast!"

Well that was enough for Mr Greedy. He opened his eyes and said to Mr Mischief: "You've played a trick on me!"

"But have I?" said Mr Mischief. "You know so much about food, that I couldn't catch you out. You guessed the right answer each time! That means there's only one thing left to do … and you know what that is, don't you?"

"Yes I do!" said Mr Greedy, rubbing his tummy. "Now it really is time to eat the food!"

Which is what he did, as fast as he could, just in case Mr Mischief played another trick on him!

Mr Happy and

It was a very windy day. It was so windy that leaves were blowing off the trees, and people's umbrellas were being blown inside out.

When Mr Happy went into his garden, something black and shiny blew right past him.

"That looks like Mr Uppity's top hat!" he called out. "Will someone help me catch it?"

But no one heard him. The wind was blowing so hard that it blew the words right out of his mouth, blew them high up into the air, over his house and far away until they were no more than a tiny little whisper.

Mr Happy ran after Mr Uppity's hat all on his own. He ran as fast as he could. He ran so fast that he was soon out of breath, and his smile started to turn down at the corners.

But then, just when he was about to give up, an extra big gust of wind blew him right off his feet. Up, up and up he went. Over the houses. Over the trees. Then down again. And there, lying just in front of him was Mr Uppity's shiny black top hat.

Mr Happy picked it up. He held on to it as tightly as he could because he didn't want the wind to blow it away again.

the windy day

Mr Happy went straight to Mr Uppity's house and rang his doorbell.
RING! RING! He waited. No reply.
He rang the bell again, three times.
RING! RING! RINGGG!

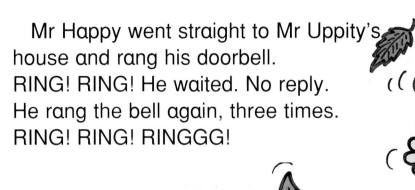

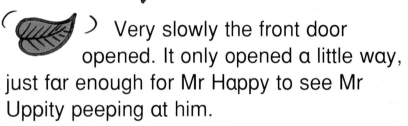 Very slowly the front door opened. It only opened a little way, just far enough for Mr Happy to see Mr Uppity peeping at him.

"What do you want?" snapped Mr Uppity, rather rudely.

Mr Happy held the top hat in front of him. Before he could say a single word, Mr Uppity flung the door wide open and snatched the hat!

"I thought I had lost my hat for good," said Mr Uppity. "Where did you find it?"

Mr Happy told him what had happened.

"Well, I'm jolly glad you did find my hat," said Mr Uppity. "I can't go anywhere without it. I've been miserable all day long – but now you have cheered me up!"

And with that, Mr Uppity put his hat on his head, held his chin up high and walked off along his garden path.

"Mind the wind doesn't blow it off again," called out Mr Happy.

But it was too late. The wind crept up quickly behind Mr Uppity, and blew his hat straight up into the air.

Mr Happy watched as Mr Uppity chased after it. "Oh dear," he said, in a little voice. "I think it's time I was somewhere else."

Mr Happy decided to go home. He'd had quite enough running about for one day. But when he arrived, there was a surprise waiting for him.

Caught in a tree in his garden was a balloon.

"Oh dear," said Mr Happy. "A lost balloon."

Mr Happy climbed the tree. He reached out to the balloon, grabbed hold of the string and … the strongest gust of wind he had felt all day blew and blew and blew. It blew Mr Happy and the balloon out of the tree. He held on to the balloon string as tightly as he could.

Up, up and up he went. Over the houses. Over the trees. Then down again …

… He landed right back where he had started, at Mr Uppity's house!

Unfortunately he landed in a prickly bush.

POP! went the balloon.

"OUCH!" said Mr Happy.

Mr Uppity came out to see what was going on. He seemed very pleased about something.

"Look," said Mr Uppity, pointing to his head.

"I got my top hat back!"

Sure enough, there without a shadow of a doubt, was Mr Uppity's shiny black top hat, perched carefully on top of his head, right where it belonged.

Just to make certain that the wind didn't blow it off again, Mr Happy tied one end of the balloon string to Mr Uppity's top hat. He gave him the other end to hold on to.

"You won't lose your hat again now," said Mr Happy.

And he was right. The next time the wind blew, up went Mr Uppity's hat - but he pulled on the string and it came straight back down again!

Little Miss Twins

In Twoland you will find two the same of everything. There are two red cars, two blue cars; two big boats, two little boats; two moons at night, and two suns in the day.

This is where Little Miss Twin and Little Miss Twin live. They're identical in every way, like two peas in a pod, two birds in a bush, or two stars in the sky. It's hard to tell the twins apart. Can you imagine how confusing that is?

Little Miss Greedy had a great time at their party. She would, wouldn't she? There were two huge chocolate cakes, and two enormous apple pies; two gigantic wobbly jellies, and two brilliant birthday cakes.

"Help yourself yourself," said the Little Miss Twins. (Isn't it funny how people who live in Twoland say the last word of a sentence twice?)

Little Miss Greedy didn't need to be asked twice. But not even she could manage to eat everything. She left two tiny crumbs on her plate. "I'm saving those for later," she said.

Then there were two loud knocks on the front door of Twotimes Cottage. KNOCK! KNOCK!

"Oh good good! Someone else has come to our party party!" the twins said together. But when they opened the door, there was no one there.

"That's funny funny," they said. "We're sure someone really did knock on the door door." Then there were two more knocks, even louder than before. KNOCK!! KNOCK!!

The Little Miss Twins went to the back door. It looked exactly the same as the front door of Twotimes Cottage. Two letterboxes, two door handles … and two keyholes. And who should be peeping in through both keyholes at the same time, but Mr Nosey.

"What's going on here?" he asked, nosily. The Little Miss Twins invited him to come inside Twotimes cottage and that was the last they saw of him for the rest of the day.

Mr Nosey was so nosey he couldn't stop opening doors and drawers, books and boxes, cupboards and cabinets. And because there were two of everything inside Twotimes Cottage, Mr Nosey quickly forgot what he'd looked at inside, and what he hadn't! And so he started all over again … and then again … and again! You wouldn't expect him to do anything else, would you?

Mr Clumsy's

Mr Clumsy had gone to watch a football match. As you probably know, Mr Clumsy is very, very clumsy. If something can go wrong, then Mr Clumsy makes sure that it does. However, the good thing about Mr Clumsy is that he doesn't seem to mind. He just smiles and carries on.

Well, there he was, minding his own business, watching the football match … when Mr Bump bumped into the goalpost.

Now Mr Bump's team needed someone to take his place. And guess who they picked?

Well, as you can imagine, Mr Clumsy isn't really the best person to be picked to play football.

The first thing he did was run onto the pitch and kick the ball so hard it burst. BANG!

Luckily for Mr Clumsy there was another football, but for some reason no one wanted to kick it to him.

"You go and be goalkeeper," said Mr Tickle.

Mr Clumsy soon got fed up being all on his own in the goal. He started to jump up and down, just to see if he could touch the top of the goalpost. Then he decided to swing from the goalpost. That was a big mistake. The goalpost creaked then snapped in half. Mr Clumsy tumbled to the ground. And soon he was all knotted up inside the net!

game of football

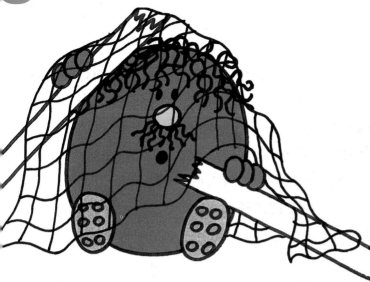

After Mr Strong had mended the goal, Mr Bump came back on to finish the rest of the game.

"I think I'll go and sit down," said Mr Clumsy.

"Why don't you be our cheerleader?" said Mr Tickle. "Then you can jump up and down as much as you like."

And that was exactly what Mr Clumsy did. He jumped up and down, did cartwheels, clapped his hands and sang songs.

All went well until he got fed up again. When he pressed a button on an electric lawnmower, off it went, zig-zagging all over the football pitch with him holding on to it.

And that was the end of the football match. Everyone ran off, leaving Mr Clumsy to cut the grass in his own clumsy way.

25

Mr Dizzy in Cleverland

Cleverland is the place where clever people live. And clever worms. And clever pigs. And even clever elephants.

They spend their time asking each other really tricky questions, such as: 'What is the opposite of black?' and: 'What's big and grey and has big ears and a trunk?' If you can answer these questions, then you could live in Cleverland too.

Now, it so happens that there is one person who lives in Cleverland who is not quite so clever. It's Mr Dizzy. He thinks orange is the opposite of black! And he thinks a big grey animal with a trunk is a mouse!

It's no use asking why Mr Dizzy lives in Cleverland. He just does. He lives in a rather dizzy house, which he built himself. It's on the side of a hill. It looks as though it might slide down the hill at any moment. If his house had a name it would be called Crooked Cottage, or Wonky Cottage, or Tipsy Cottage.

For instance, the front door leans so much that Mr Dizzy has to lean right over to go through it. And if he leans over too much … he falls flat on his face!

For example, when Mr Dizzy turns the tap on in his bath, the water fills up at one end only and then pours out over the edge. It goes straight through the ceiling … and into the kitchen sink, which is where he ends up having his bath!

One day Mr Dizzy decided to go for a walk. Before he set off he looked out of his bedroom window, to see what the weather was doing. "Looks like it might rain. Must remember to take my umbrella," he said. But by the time he got downstairs he'd forgotten what he'd just said – so he went walking without his umbrella. And his raincoat. And his wellington boots.

Just as Mr Dizzy reached the bottom of the hill it began to rain. Only in Cleverland the rain doesn't fall in tiny drops, or little spots, or teeny splashes. In Cleverland the rain falls in great big drops as big as puddles. Which meant, of course, that Mr Dizzy got rather wet. Everyone else put up their umbrellas, and put on their raincoats and wellington boots. They didn't get wet at all. How very clever of them.

But as for Mr Dizzy, he held out his arms and jumped into as many puddles as he could find. Did he mind getting so wet? Not at all! "This is the best bath I've had all week!" he said.

After the rain stopped he saw a notice on a tree.

It said:

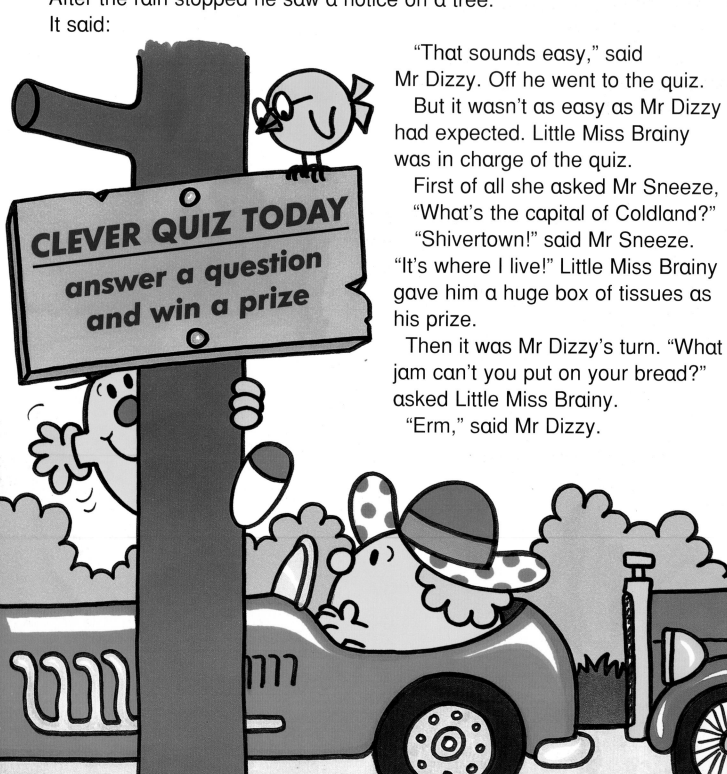

CLEVER QUIZ TODAY

answer a question and win a prize

"That sounds easy," said Mr Dizzy. Off he went to the quiz.

But it wasn't as easy as Mr Dizzy had expected. Little Miss Brainy was in charge of the quiz.

First of all she asked Mr Sneeze, "What's the capital of Coldland?"

"Shivertown!" said Mr Sneeze. "It's where I live!" Little Miss Brainy gave him a huge box of tissues as his prize.

Then it was Mr Dizzy's turn. "What jam can't you put on your bread?" asked Little Miss Brainy.

"Erm," said Mr Dizzy.

"Hurry up," said Little Miss Brainy.

Just at that moment everyone heard a car horn. PEEP! PEEP! it went. And again. And again.

It was Mr Funny in his car. He was stuck behind Mr Strong in his car, who was stuck behind Little Miss Splendid in her car. They were all coming to the quiz.

Suddenly Mr Dizzy shouted "I know the answer! It was a trick question. You can't put traffic jam on your bread!" Which, of course, was the right answer.

Guess what Little Miss Brainy gave Mr Dizzy for his prize. It was a certificate. It said:

Mr Dizzy
Cleverest person I know

But you know, don't you, that if she'd asked him what the opposite of black was, he'd have said orange … or blue … or green!

PEEP! PEEP!

Dandelion counting

Little Miss Fickle lived in Dandelion Cottage. She had wanted to call it Rose Cottage, but then she had changed her mind. She thought Tulip Cottage might sound better. But then she had changed her mind again and decided to call it Chrysanthemum Cottage.

Now she liked the sound of that most of all, but by the time she had learned to say it properly, her garden had grown full of dandelions. There wasn't a rose, tulip or chrysanthemum in sight. So she called her house Dandelion Cottage instead.

One day she was counting all her dandelions, when along

came Little Miss Stubborn. "Coo-ee, Little Miss Stubborn," called out Little Miss Fickle. "Come over here please." "No!" said Little Miss Stubborn. "Well, I'll come over to you then," said Little Miss Fickle.

Which is just what she did. "I'd like to ask you a favour," she said to Little Miss Stubborn. "I've been counting all my dandelions, and I can't decide if I've got two hundred and five, or five hundred and two. I was wondering if you'd count them with me."

"Oh, I'm far too busy for that," said Little Miss Stubborn. "Far too busy indeed."

Just at that moment along came Little Miss Greedy. "Hello," she said. "My, your garden looks lovely with all those dandelions," she said to Little Miss Fickle.

"Does it?" asked Little Miss Fickle. "Is it really lovely?"

"It's the loveliest dandelion garden I know," said Little Miss Greedy. "It's so lovely, I could spend all day looking at it."

"Well," began Little Miss Fickle, "If you think it's that nice, maybe you'd like to help me find out how many dandelions I've got."

"Er…" began Little Miss Greedy.

"And if you're very lucky you might find the big chocolate cake that I've hidden in the garden," said Little Miss Fickle.

"I'll start right away!" said Little Miss Greedy. So off she ran.

"Did you say chocolate cake?" asked Little Miss Stubborn, quietly. "Well, maybe I could help you count your dandelions, after all," she said.

But, oh, dear! What a sight they saw when they got into Little Miss Fickle's garden. Little Miss Greedy was trampling all over the dandelions looking for the chocolate cake.

"I've looked everywhere," said Little Miss Greedy. "There's no chocolate cake here."

"Oh, well, I must have changed my mind and left it somewhere else," said Little Miss Fickle. That was the worst thing she could have said, wasn't it? Off ran Little Miss Greedy, quickly followed by Little Miss Stubborn.

"Hey, come back," called out Little Miss Fickle. "You haven't counted my dandelions yet!" she shouted after them.

But you can count them for her, can't you?

Mr Sneeze in Coldland

Mr Sneeze lives in a far away country called Coldland. It's so cold that people who live there don't need fridges or freezers in which to keep their food. They can leave ice creams, and ice lollies, and ice cubes on their kitchen tables all day long, and they won't melt.

Mr Sneeze's cottage is in a town called Shivertown. It's a pretty little cottage which is always covered in snow.

Every morning, Mr Sneeze looks out of his bedroom window, and every morning the same thing happens. He sneezes … not once … not twice … but three times, very quickly, one after the other.

His first sneeze is quite small: "Atishoo." His second sneeze is louder: "Atish-OO." His third sneeze is the loudest of all: "A-TISH-OO!", at which point the cottage shivers and shudders, and all the snow slides off the roof and lands in the garden.
It makes a loud thudding noise
as it hits the ground. THUD!

Mr Sneeze's garden isn't a garden with green grass, or red flowers, or brown trees. It's a snow garden with white snowmen, which Mr Sneeze is very good at making, white snowdrops, white snowdrifts and lots of white snowballs.

One morning, after he'd sneezed the snow off the roof, he went into his snow garden. And do you know what he saw? First, he saw something orange and twisty coming out from underneath the fallen snow. It looked like it might be someone's long bendy arm. Then he saw something pink and round bulging up through the snow. It looked like it might be someone's big round tummy.

Mr Sneeze felt like he was going to sneeze again. It felt like it was going to be a much bigger sneeze than before.

"A-TISH-OOO!" sneezed Mr Sneeze. This sneeze was so big that it blew all the snow off the ground and back up onto the roof of his cottage. THUD!

And who do you think he found lying under the snow?

The long bendy arm belonged to Mr Tickle, and the big round tummy belonged to Mr Greedy.

What a surprise they got when all the snow slithered off the roof of Mr Sneeze's cottage. It had covered them from top to toe.

And now they were so cold their feet felt like blocks of ice, and their noses were beginning to itch.

"Oh dear," said Mr Tickle. "I think we're catching Coldland colds."

"And I'm starting to feel hungry," said Mr Greedy, who was patting his big empty tummy.

"You can have a plate of frozen peas and a glass of orange iceade," said Mr Sneeze. "Or a freezing fishcake and an ice cube to suck."

"YUCK!" said Mr Greedy, who didn't like the sound of that.

Just then, Mr Sneeze started to scrunch up his eyes. His mouth started to open … wide, then wider still. His nose began to twitch, and his head began to shake a little.

"Oh no!" called out Mr Tickle. He's going to sneeze again!"

"A-TISH-OOO-OOO!" sneezed Mr Sneeze, even louder and longer than before.

Mr Tickle looked up at the snow on the roof of the cottage. It was still there. It hadn't moved. Not so much as one teeny, weeny little flake of snow had fallen down this time.

"Phew!" said Mr Tickle, holding up his long bendy arms, ready to catch any snow that did fall.

Mr Greedy didn't say anything. But his big, round, empty, hungry tummy did. First it said: "Blu-rrp," followed by "GRR-UMPH," and then, just in case no one had heard it the first time: "BLU-RRP!"

That did it. The last noisy tummy rumble was enough to shake the snow on the roof … and down it started to slide, past the chimney, over the roof tiles, past Mr Sneeze's bedroom window, and into the snow garden below. THUD!

Mr Tickle and Mr Greedy didn't wait for the snow to hit the ground. They ran, and skated, and slid away as fast as they could, back to somewhere warm.

As for Mr Sneeze, well, he'd still got the whole of the day to make more snowmen for his snow garden! What a lovely start to his day.

Little Miss Busy and

Little Miss Busy is always as busy as a bee. She isn't happy unless she is busy.

For instance, when Mr Sneeze runs out of tissues, she makes herself as busy as she can by dashing off to his house to fetch not one, but one hundred and one tissues! When she sees Little Miss Tidy all on her own tidying up after a messy party, she makes herself so busy that in no time at all everything is neat and tidy again.

One day, Little Miss Busy went for a walk in the park. She felt like being busy, but she couldn't decide what to do.

Just then she saw a horseshoe lying in the grass. It gave her an idea. "Well," she said, out loud, "I know that horseshoes are supposed to be lucky. Who can I give this horseshoe to, so they can have lots of good luck?"

Little Miss Busy picked up the horseshoe and said, "Little Miss Brainy could do with some good luck today!" So, feeling busy, off she went to see her clever friend.

Today was a special day for Little Miss Brainy. To show just how brainy she was, she was answering lots of different questions all day long. The trouble was, she wasn't very good at it.

the lucky horseshoe

For instance, when Little Miss Greedy asked her to guess how many jam doughnuts she had eaten for breakfast, Little Miss Brainy didn't know the answer. When Little Miss Magic asked her how many letter a's there were in 'abracadabra', Little Miss Brainy counted the letter b's instead. And when Little Miss Somersault asked her what the difference was between a handstand and a hatstand, Little Miss Brainy got all muddled up and said, "You hang hats on a handstand!"

Just at that moment Little Miss Busy arrived with the lucky horseshoe. "I've brought you a lovely surprise," she said to Little Miss Brainy. "This lucky horseshoe will bring you lots of good luck. Now you'll get all the answers right!"

Little Miss Brainy took the horseshoe. She held it tightly in both hands. Then she started to smile.

"Does anyone have another question for me?" she asked.

"Yes, I do," said little Miss Greedy, again. "How many eggs did I have for breakfast?"

Little Miss Brainy thought hard. "Mmm," she said, "I think I know the answer. You ate seventeen boiled eggs. Am I right?"

Little Miss Greedy could scarcely believe her ears.

"That's absolutely right!" she said, in complete amazement.

Then it was Little Miss Magic's turn.

"What can you hold without touching it?" she said.

Little Miss Brainy looked puzzled. She held the lucky horseshoe more tightly than before and said, "Your breath! Am I right?"

Little Miss Magic could hardly believe that Little Miss Brainy had given the correct answer to such a tricky question.

Last of all, Little Miss Somersault asked her what the difference was

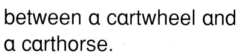

between a cartwheel and a carthorse.

"That's a funny question," said Little Miss Brainy.
She began to think. "Mmm," she said.

But before she could answer, Little Miss Busy called out, "Look! A horse! It's lost one of it's shoes. In fact, I think it's lost this horseshoe," she said, pointing to the lucky horseshoe.

Little Miss Busy felt like being busy again, so she took the horseshoe to the horse, who was very pleased to have it back.

"I'm still waiting for an answer to my question," said Little Miss Somersault.

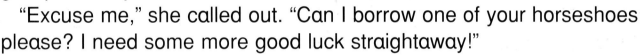

But without the lucky horseshoe, Little Miss Brainy didn't know the answer.

"Mmm," Little Miss Brainy said again. Then, quick as a flash, she ran after the horse as it galloped away.

"Excuse me," she called out. "Can I borrow one of your horseshoes please? I need some more good luck straightaway!"

That was the last anyone saw of Little Miss Brainy that day.

"Well," said Little Miss Busy. "Fancy that. What a busy day it's been after all. I've helped Little Miss Brainy and a horse today. How busy I've been!"

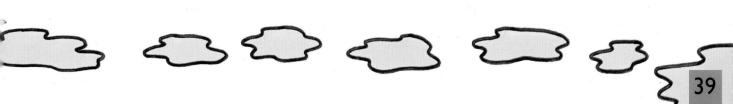

Little Miss Contrary in Muddleland

Muddleland is a very mixed-up place. Or as they say in Muddleland, it's a very muxed-ip place.

For instance, in Muddleland worms live in trees, and birds live in holes in the ground. For example, cars fly in the sky, and aeroplanes drive along the roads. As for the people who live in Muddleland, well, they never know if they are coming and going, or going and coming.

Little Miss Contrary lives in Muddleland. She would, wouldn't she? If you ask her to sing a song, she stands on her head. And if you ask her to count to ten, she tells you the time instead. You see, Little Miss Contrary always does the opposite of what you expect her to do.

One day, Little Miss Contrary had a cold.

"Oh good, a warm!" she said.

What she meant to say was: "Oh no, a cold," but, of course, it didn't come out like that.

She started to look for her tissues. She found them in a

cornflake box. And guess what she found in the tissue box. Cornflakes. Lots of old, soggy cornflakes.

She poured milk on the tissues … and blew her nose on the cornflakes! What a muddle she was in.

She turned on the radio. And tried to put a slice of bread into it. She thought it was the toaster!

"It's going to be a wet and windy day," said the weatherman on the radio.

"A warm and sunny day!" repeated Little Miss Contrary, saying exactly the opposite.

She looked out of her window. Leaves were blowing off the trees. Umbrellas were flapping inside out.

She put on a pair of sunglasses and went into her garden … and was blown off her feet by a big gust of wind. She landed in a tree.

Next to a worm, of course.

The next gust of wind blew her onto the roof of her house and straight down her chimney! She was covered from head to toe in black soot.

"I'm having a very good day!" she said, but what she should have said was "I'm not having a very good day!"

She decided to have a bath, to wash the soot off. But instead she climbed into bed. And fell fast asleep, which was probably the best place for her! Wasn't it?

Mr Happy

Mr Happy lives in Happyland. He couldn't possibly live anywhere else, could he? For instance, you wouldn't find him living in a place called Unhappyland, would you?

Mr Happy only wants to live in the happiest land there is, with lots of other happy, smiling people. In Happyland everyone smiles and feels happy all day long. Even the cats and dogs, worms and snails, birds and bees are happy in Happyland. And the flowers. And even the weeds. And the trees, too. In fact, the trees feel so happy that they grow higher … and higher … and higher … until you can't see the tops of them. They must be at least one hundred feet tall!

There's something else special about Happyland, too. The sun shines all day long. It only rains at night, when Mr Happy is tucked up, fast asleep in his bed.

Lucky Mr Happy! He can play outside all day every day because the weather is always bright and sunny – just like he is! No wonder he's such a happy person!

Mr Happy lives in a little cottage by a lovely lake. He wakes up early every morning, and the first thing he does is pull back his bedroom curtains and look out of the window.

He looks across to the mountains on the other side of the lake. As the sun comes up from behind them, Mr Happy's smile turns up at the corners of his mouth and grows bigger … and bigger … and bigger. It's the best start to a happy new day in Happyland!

Now, one morning, not long ago, something very unusual happened. Mr Happy was waiting for the sun to start shining. He waited. And carried on waiting. His smile began to crinkle up on his lips. He started to look a little bit unhappy.

"This is very strange," he said. "I'll go and see what's happening."

Outside, on the shore at the edge of the lake, a crowd of cats and dogs, worms and snails, birds and bees had gathered. They were looking at something in the sky. Mr Happy looked, too.

"Oh," he said, quickly followed by: "Mmm," and then: "Well, I never!"

High above the hundred-foot-tall trees, and above the tips of the

tallest mountains, in the very place where the sun should have been, there was a fluffy white cloud. And coming out of the cloud was the brightest, the most colourful, the biggest rainbow you could ever imagine. Mr Happy opened his eyes as wide as saucers, and his smile stretched from ear to ear. He'd never seen a rainbow in Happyland before.

Now you might think that it's impossible to catch a rainbow. And that's perfectly true of course, but as you know, Happyland is where the happiest of things can happen. So, when Mr Happy cupped his hands together and held them out, it didn't surprise him that the rainbow simply jumped into them!

Mr Happy began to walk away from the lake, back up the winding path to his cottage. He walked very carefully, and quite slowly, taking great care not to let go of the rainbow.

Every few steps, Mr Happy
stopped and looked over his shoulder.
He saw that the fluffy cloud was moving too, and as
it moved, Mr Happy saw something peeping out from
behind it.

By the
time Mr Happy
reached his house, the
rainbow had grown paler and
paler until he wasn't sure if it was
there at all. He looked for the cloud, but
that had vanished too, over the mountains
and far away. And in its place, just where it
should have been all along, was the early morning
sun, shining warm and bright.

"Hurray!" said Mr Happy. "It's
going to be another happy day
in Happyland."

The End

Mr. Chatterbox

Mr. Clumsy

Mr. Daydream

little Miss Fickle

Mr. Mischief

Mr. Uppity

Mr. Dizzy

little Miss Somersault

Mr. Greedy

little Miss Scatterbrain

Mr. Mean

little Miss Stubborn

little Miss Magic

Mr. Tickle

Mr. Happy

little Miss Greedy

Mr. Sneeze

Mr. Nosey

little Miss Twins

Mr. Strong

Mr. Grumble

Mr. Bump

Mr. Forgetful

little Miss Contrary